AF488475

THE ROYAL PLAY PARTY

SAPPHIRE CITY SERIES

BOOK FOUR

IRELAND LORELEI

Phoenix Voices Publishing

Copyright © 2024 by Ireland Lorelei

All rights reserved.

No part of this publication may be reproduced, distributed, or transmitted in any form or by any means, including photocopying, recording, or other electronic or mechanical methods, without the prior written permission of the publisher, except as permitted by U.S. copyright law. For permission requests, contact Phoenix Voices Publishing, 7901 4th St. N, St. Petersburg, FL, 33702, 727-222-0090.

The story, all names, characters, and incidents portrayed in this production are fictitious. No identification with actual persons (living or deceased), places, buildings, and products is intended or should be inferred.

Ireland Lorelei asserts the moral right to be identified as the author of this work.

Ireland Lorelei has no responsibility for the persistence or accuracy of URLs for external or third-party Internet Websites referred to in this publication and does not guarantee that any content on such Websites is, or will remain, accurate or appropriate.

Designations used by companies to distinguish their products are often claimed as trademarks. All brand names and product names used in this book and on its cover are trade names, service marks, trademarks, and registered trademarks of their respective owners. The publishers and the book are not associated with any product or vendor mentioned in this book. None of the companies referenced within the book have endorsed the book.

CONTENTS

Note To Readers

The characters in this book are unapologetic and dramatic. The scenes are steamy and the road to happily ever after maybe twisted. This book is meant for audiences 18 years old and older.

A Cinderella Remake

Cinderella is one of my favorite fairy tales. I have remade this story to be one that brings a little smut, kinkiness, and fetishes to the story. This remake is not for children but is for grown women who love to read smut and have their own kinky fantasies that some may or may not indulge themselves with!

This is not your old Cinderella story by any means. You will see more in this remake than just the kink and smut! I think it makes for an interesting story.

So, get ready to be amazed! Picture yourself as Isabella!

CHAPTER ONE

Isabella

Today, I am sitting in the quiet solitude of my bedroom, surrounded by the faint echoes of memories; I find myself reflecting on the intricate tapestry of my life. It's as though the room itself holds the whispers of my past, weaving a tale that began long ago in the warmth of family and love.

Growing up in Sapphire City has its pros and cons, like anywhere else, I am sure. But the King and Queen who rule our little kingdom are amazing. They always do their best to make sure everyone in the city has a job that makes them enough wages to provide for their families and that there is enough food for all. For the people that work for them, they go above and beyond. Both of my parents served the King and Queen their entire lives. They actually met at the palace. My mother was the prince's nanny, and my father was the head security guard. I remember my mother being able to take me to work with her, and even after her death, they allowed my father to take me to the new nanny to watch until he remarried. So, I guess you could say that the prince was my first friend. I believe that this is why my stepmother hates me. Anyway, after my father's death, the King and Queen made sure that our family was well taken care of, which left my stepmother not having to work.

I remember the days when laughter echoed through the halls of my home, a sweet melody that resonated with the joy of childhood. But, like a haunting refrain, those days are now distant echoes, overshadowed by the weight of time, death, and circumstances.

My journey into this life of humble servitude commenced with the departure of the sunniest figure in my existence. I was only seven years old when my mother, my pillar of strength, succumbed to the cruelty of cancer. Her death left a void, a void that seemed insurmountable for my father, desperate to find a woman who would be able to give me the same motherly love, protection, and advice, someone to teach me how to be a woman. So, when I turned nine years old, my father made a decision that would alter the course of my destiny. Seeking to provide me with the maternal guidance he believed I needed, he remarried.

Lady Helena, a woman of poise but concealed cunning, entered our lives with the promise of a new beginning. Little did I know that this new beginning would unfold into a horror movie of my life that mirrored the darkest tales told by the flickering flames of the hearth.

My stepsisters, Anna and Dressie, were told to be reluctant companions of my daily existence after my father died. They were bestowed upon me as siblings, though the bonds of sisterhood remained elusive in the eyes of their mother; we became sisters in all the ways that mattered. The dynamics within the walls of our home were transforming, forging a reality that bore no resemblance to the fairy tales I once believed in.

When we were in the presence of Lady Helena, my sisters had to act a certain way, even though in our alone times, the three of us made a pact that no matter what their mother made them do, I had to know that it wasn't their choice and that they loved me. So, Anna, with her gawky charm and misplaced confidence, cast shadows of disdain over my every step, and Dressie, possessing a sharp tongue and a penchant for cruelty, seemed determined to erase any trace of my mother's influence that lingered within our home. The three of us, thrust together by familial ties, navigated the precarious dance of coexistence under the watchful eyes of Lady Helena.

My father unwittingly wed a woman whose heart was colder than the winds on the highest mountaintop during the winter months. He became an unwitting participant in the unfolding drama. Blinded by his own desires for a peaceful household, he failed to see the subtle shifts in power, the undercurrents of resentment that flowed beneath the surface.

As I sit in my room, surrounded by the remnants of a childhood long gone, I can't help but wonder how I can escape this life. The flickering candlelight casts shadows on the worn pages of my story; each line etched with the pain of loss, betrayal, and the quiet resilience that defines my existence.

The memories unfold like a worn tapestry before my eyes, revealing the threads of joy and sorrow that have woven the intricate pattern of my life. In the quiet of this room, where my dreams were once as boundless as the stars, I find solace in the fragments of a fairy tale beginning that led me to this very moment.

My father, a gentle soul whose eyes mirrored the kindness etched in his heart, became both the architect of my new life and an unwitting pawn in the unfolding narrative. The loss of my mother cast a perpetual shadow over our home, and in his quest to bring sunlight back into my world, he sought solace in the form of Lady Helena.

Initially, hope danced in his eyes, fueled by the prospect of a harmonious family. Yet, as the days turned into years, the reality of our domestic realm shifted. Lady Helena's graceful exterior concealed a calculated demeanor, and my father, ever eager to preserve tranquility, seemed oblivious to the subtle transformation within our walls.

Our interactions, once marked by shared laughter and familial warmth, became stilted under the watchful eyes of my stepmother and stepsisters. Lady Helena's influence seemed to tighten its grip, and my father, perhaps out of an earnest desire for familial unity, was inadvertently ensnared in her designs.

As my days became a symphony of chores and muted conversations, I often caught glimpses of my father's internal conflict. His eyes, once alive with the sparkle of a doting parent, now mirrored the silent struggle between his obligations as a husband and his responsibilities as a father. The lines etched on his forehead bore witness to the weight he carried, a burden he unknowingly placed upon himself in his pursuit of a peaceful household.

Despite the strain on our relationship, there were moments when the veil of Lady Helena's influence momentarily lifted, and my father and I could share fleeting moments of connection. In those stolen seconds, he would offer a reassuring smile or a quiet nod, silently communicating a shared understanding of the oppressive atmosphere within our home.

Yet, the tenuous threads that bound us began to fray as the chasm between Lady Helena's ambitions and our family's well-being widened. My father's efforts to maintain peace inadvertently distanced him from the daughter who yearned for the love and security that once defined our home.

I grapple today with the complexity of my relationship with my father. He, too, was a victim of the choices made in the wake of loss, and as I reflected on our shared history, I couldn't help but harbor a bittersweet affection for the man whose intentions were noble but whose actions unwittingly led us down this winding path.

My heart carried both gratitude for the moments of understanding and sorrow for the silent witness my father had become to the metamorphosis of our once joy-filled home into a realm dominated by shadows of duty and unspoken compromise. The family that once was had disappeared due to the delicate intricacies of familial bonds strained under the weight of unforeseen circumstances.

The day of my father's death marked the unraveling of the fragile threads that held our "family" together. His sudden departure left me engulfed in a profound sense of loss as if the very foundation of my world had crumbled beneath my feet.

The once familiar rooms echoed with a haunting emptiness, and the absence of his reassuring smile turned our dwelling into a cavern of solitude. Lady Helena, who had been a figure of subtle influence, now emerged as the harbinger of a malevolent transformation. In the wake of my father's death, her true nature unfurled like the petals of a poisonous flower.

No longer bound by the constraints of a husband's benevolence, Lady Helena morphed into an embodiment of cruelty, a wicked force that cast a malevolent shadow over my existence. The love and understanding my father had offered in fleeting moments were replaced by an unrelenting tyranny, and the home that once held traces of warmth transformed into a realm governed by coldness and calculated malice.

Anna and Dressie were still walking the thin line between Lady Helena's cruelty towards me and their love for me. They mourned my father as much as I did. He never treated them any differently from me, unlike their mother did me. Lady Helena made the mourning period brief and swiftly replaced it with an oppressive atmosphere that seemed to revel in my vulnerability.

Gone were the days of shared glances and unspoken understanding. Lady Helena, now an evil enchantress in my life's narrative, orchestrated a symphony of torment, ensuring that every moment was steeped in misery. The house, once a haven, became a prison of despair, and I, the unwitting captive, bore the brunt of her newfound malevolence.

In the solitude of my room, I found refuge in the memories of a time when my father's love shielded me from the harsh realities of the world. Now, bereft of his protection, I navigated the treacherous waters of Lady Helena's cruelty, my heart heavy with the burden of grief and the weight of unspoken longing.

The life I had once envisioned, filled with dreams of joy and love, now seemed like a distant mirage, a fleeting illusion shattered by the cruel hands of fate. Lady Helena, the evil stepmother, reveled in her newfound dominion.

As I faced the harsh reality of life after my father's death, I clung to the fragments of my past, desperately searching for traces of the innocence and warmth that had defined our family. Yet, in the oppressive grasp of Lady Helena's cruelty, I couldn't escape the chilling realization that my life had warped into a nightmare, and I was left to navigate a world transformed into a sinister tapestry of despair.

Chapter Two

As I walk through the garden in the back of the palace, the weight of nostalgia settles upon me like a heavy cloak. Memories, both cherished and fraught with complexity, flood my mind, painting a vivid tableau of my journey thus far. At twenty-eight years old, I am the prince of Sapphire City, heir to the throne, yet my identity is shrouded in layers of secrecy and contradiction.

Ever since I graduated from college, my parents, the King and Queen, have been riding me to find a wife and settle down. They have no idea how hard that is for me. For one, I am a prince and finding someone who doesn't let the title go to their head is hard. Second, because of my secret sexual fetishes, it makes it even harder.

Growing up within the hallowed halls of the palace, I was enveloped in a world of privilege and expectation. My father and my mother ruled with a firm yet benevolent hand, guiding me with love and wisdom. Our relationship was one of mutual respect, tempered by the weight of duty and the legacy of our royal lineage.

From an early age, the weight of expectation bore down upon me, shaping my path and molding my character. Yet, amidst the rigid protocols and formalities of royal life, there existed moments of warmth and intimacy with my parents. They were my pillars of strength, the anchors that tethered me to the realm of reality amidst the tumultuous currents of palace intrigue.

I remember having one friend as a young child, a girl named Bella. Her mother was my nanny until she died, and my parents allowed her to bring her daughter with her. I remember that we would play in this very garden. We were so young! I remember telling her that she would be my queen and help me run my kingdom! She was beautiful even then. She had golden blond curls that bounced when she walked and the most beautiful blue eyes. I remember thinking that I could set sail in her eyes. They were as blue as the deepest ocean.

I don't know what happened to her. After her mother passed, her father would still bring her with him when he came to work. He was one of our security guards, the head-to-be, now that I think about it. He was always with my father wherever he went. I wonder if I will ever see Bella again.

I reminisce about my youth attending boarding school in England. The memories flood back with clarity. It was a period of my life marked by a potent blend of excitement, trepidation, and the inexorable pull of newfound independence.

Stepping onto the grounds of the prestigious institution, I was acutely aware of the weight of expectation that rested upon my shoulders. As the prince of Sapphire City, my every move was scrutinized; my actions were a reflection of my family's legacy. Yet, amidst the palpable aura of privilege that permeated the air, I found myself yearning for a taste of normalcy, a respite from the suffocating confines of royal protocol.

The initial days were a whirlwind of introductions and orientations as I navigated the labyrinthine corridors of the school with a mixture of awe and trepidation. The students, a diverse tapestry of backgrounds and experiences, welcomed me with a curiosity tempered by deference. I was no longer Prince James, heir to the throne, but simply James, a boy eager to carve out his own path amidst the hallowed halls of academia.

The rigors of academic life demanded my attention, and I threw myself into my studies with a fervor born of determination. Yet, it was the camaraderie of my peers that truly defined my experience at boarding school. Bonds forged in the crucible of shared experiences, friendships that transcended the boundaries of class and privilege.

Together, we navigated the intricacies of school life, from the relentless demands of coursework to the exhilarating freedom of weekend excursions into the heart of London. The city, with its bustling streets and vibrant culture, became our playground. It was a canvas upon which we painted memories that would endure long after our time at boarding school had come to an end.

Yet, amidst the laughter and camaraderie, there existed moments of solitude and introspection. As the prince, I was keenly aware of the weight of my responsibilities, the burden of expectation that lay heavy upon my shoulders. In the quiet solitude of my room, I grappled with the dichotomy of my existence, a boy torn between duty and desire, tradition and rebellion.

It was during those quiet moments that I sought solace in the written word, losing myself in the pages of books that offered escape from the confines of reality. Literature became my sanctuary, a refuge from the tumultuous currents of royal life that threatened to engulf me at every turn.

Yet, even as I immersed myself in the pursuit of knowledge, a part of me longed for something more, a sense of purpose that transcended the trappings of royalty. It was a desire that simmered beneath the surface, a flickering ember waiting to be ignited into flame.

In the hallowed halls of boarding school, I discovered facets of myself that lay dormant beneath the veneer of royal obligation. I forged friendships that would endure the test of time, and I confronted challenges that tested the very limits of my resolve. It was a transformative experience, one that shaped the man I would become, a man who would one day rule over Sapphire City with a wisdom born of humility and empathy.

As I reflect upon those formative years, I am filled with a profound sense of gratitude for the opportunities afforded to me. Boarding school in England was more than just an education; it was a crucible in which I forged the foundations of my identity, laying the groundwork for the journey that lay ahead. And though the memories may fade with time, the lessons learned, and the friendships forged will endure as enduring reminders of my life that will forever hold a special place in my heart.

My parents allowed me to go off to college in the United States. Harvard offered a brief respite from the constraints of royal life. It was a time of exploration and self-discovery, a period marked by the heady exhilaration of newfound freedom. Yet, even in the distant shores of foreign lands, the shadow of my royal lineage followed me like a silent specter. It was never too far in the back of my mind. However, I never introduced myself as a prince, and no one other than the Registrar's Office knew that I was a prince. I was able to just be James and that is all my friends knew about me. As time moved on, I made a few best friends that I knew would always be friends, I did finally tell them the truth. Carl and Gary would become my brothers, and we would visit each other and take vacations together every chance we got.

These years were a whirlwind of hedonistic indulgence and reckless abandon. The allure of nightlife and the company of like-minded peers beckoned me into a world of excess and extravagance. The media dubbed me a playboy, a moniker that I wore with a mixture of defiance and resignation. Behind the veneer of frivolity, however, lay a secret world that few dared to explore.

BDSM! Those four letters held a power over me that, in the beginning, I struggled to comprehend. In the clandestine confines of underground clubs and private chambers, I found solace in the embrace of a lifestyle that defied societal norms. It was a realm of paradoxes where pain and pleasure intertwined in a delicate dance of submission and dominance. I found myself in those underground clubs. I found out what my fetishes, desires, and sexual kinks were. I also realized what type of woman my wife, my queen, would have to be for me to marry her.

Yet, even as I reveled in the clandestine pleasures of my hidden desires, a sense of unease gnawed at the edges of my consciousness. The weight of secrecy, the fear of exposure, cast a pall over my nocturnal escapades. I longed for a release, a moment of liberation from the shackles of my own making.

As I sit and reminisce about my college days and getting into BDSM, and how I now sneak off to England to some kink clubs, an idea came to me like a bolt of lightning illuminating the darkest recesses of my mind. While my parents are out of the country for the month, I am going to throw a Royal Play Party. I will call all my college friends and some of my friends from England who are in the lifestyle and have them come to the palace hidden away from the prying eyes of society. I would have the servants help me turn the grand ballroom into a BDSM dungeon!

Then, I will have the messengers go out into Sapphire City and invite all the men and women from ages twenty-two to thirty to come and learn about the lifestyle and hopefully partake. I really need to find a local sub, even though my parents want me to find a wife to make my princess. But little do they know that the future princess will have to be in the lifestyle and not only be my wife but my sub.

CHAPTER THREE

Lady Helena

BEING A WIDOW, EVEN in Sapphire City, was rough. When my beloved Richard passed away, my whole life changed. He left me with two little girls. Anna was eight years old, and Dressie was ten years old. He never had a prestigious job, but we had enough to live off of and to have some nice things. It didn't matter because we were madly in love. When he passed away, I know I was bitter and angry, and that has carried me through my life. It carried me to seek out my second husband, Edward. It still carries me today.

Edward was the head of the Royal Guard. I remember the first time I saw him. He was a handsome man by all accounts. But I could care less about his looks. I needed a man with money who could financially support me and my girls. From the moment I saw him in his Royal uniform, I started digging up information on him. He was a widow as well. His wife had passed away two years earlier and left him to raise a daughter about the same age as my girls. I knew then exactly what I needed to do to get his attention. I needed to use his wife's death along with my husband's death to get him to see that we could help each other. He could be the supporter that my girls and I needed, and I could be the mother his daughter needed. I never expected the arrangement in my head to not be what he would have wanted. He wanted to find love again, to have what he had with his first wife. So, I had to play my cards differently, and that meant I had to woe him. I had to make him fall in love with me, and that also meant making sure that I showed that little spoiled brat daughter of his, Isabella, that I loved her too. But no matter what, she always got what she wanted. I tried my best to fake love to them both until he finally bought it. Once we were married, I was able to show some of my true colors. I hate his spoiled little brat, and after he died, I was really able to be me.

As I stand by the window, I see the palace messenger getting out of the limo and walking up the walkway to my house. I rush to the front door and open it up before he makes it to the door to knock.

I smile and give a little flirtatious giggle, "What can I do for you today, Sir?"

The messenger replies, "I am here to deliver invitations to the three young women of the house to a party being thrown by Prince James."

My eyes narrow as he hands me the sumptuous invitations. The parchment, delicate and adorned, bears the unmistakable insignia of the Royal Palace. It looks like an exclusive affair promising some fun and excitement for the young adults in Sapphire City.

"Thank you, Sir," I tell him with another burst of giggles as he turns and walks back down the walkway. His eyes flicker with a fleeting curiosity, a question he dares not voice. It amuses me, this silent dance of those who unknowingly tread upon the stage of my grand design.

As the messenger disappears from sight, a discreet observer of the unfolding drama, I turn and walk to the back of the house and look out the window to watch the linens swaying in the breeze. Isabella, still immersed in her duties.

In this moment, I realized that I have the power to disclose the enigmatic invitation to my step-daughter, Isabella, or not, and I am not going to as I think about her diligently hanging out clothes on the clothesline in the back yard. Now, my daughters, Anna and Dressie, will get their invitations. I need one of them to catch the eye of the prince.

"Anna! Dressie!" I yell up the stairs.

"Yes, Mother," they both yell in unison as they come down the stairs.

As they walk up to me with eager eyes gleaming, I hand each of them an invitation. They look at the seal and then open them with haste. Their joy is palpable, an unfiltered manifestation of their unbridled enthusiasm at being deemed worthy of such an exclusive event. The air resonates with their animated chatter, and I, the silent orchestrator, observe as the tendrils of my influence weave through their jubilant conversations.

"Oh, Mother, this is splendid!" Anna exclaims, clutching her invitation as if it were a precious jewel.

Dressie, ever the one for dramatic flair, gushes, "Finally, the recognition we deserve. It's about time the royal court acknowledged our status."

Anna, with her endearing clumsiness, clutches the invitation as if it were a key to salvation. Dressie, embodying entitlement, revels in the adulation that accompanies this coveted document. Their enthusiasm is wonderful; it fills the air as they discuss their attire, how to make an impression, and the potential of catching the eye of the prince. It's a dialogue I subtly guide, weaving the threads of their aspirations into the intricate tapestry of my design, and have one of my daughters become Princess of Sapphire City and our next Queen. Yet, in the midst of their exuberance, there is a conspicuous silence, a deliberate omission. The unspoken truth lingers like an elusive specter, as neither Anna nor Dressie deigns to mention the presence of a third invitation, the invitation intended for Isabella. The omission, a carefully executed directive, aligns with my silent plan.

Isabella is oblivious to the joyous revelry transpiring in her absence as she continues her labor in the solitude of the backyard, dutifully fulfilling the mundane task assigned to her. The linens sway in the breeze, and she moves to the rhythm of the music playing in her Airpods.

As Anna and Dressie are swept away in their elation, I order them not to mention the third invitation. They know not to undermine me, but they don't want Isabella to go any more than I do.

"Do either of you know what a 'play party' is?" I ask them.

Anna looks at Dressie, who shrugs her shoulders. Dressie then says, "I have no idea, Mother."

"I don't either. It sounds mysterious. But whatever it is, I want the two of you to be there and for one of you to catch the eye of the prince," I tell them before I walk upstairs.

CHAPTER FOUR

Isabella

FIVE DAYS LATER — *The Day of the Party....*

As I am sweeping and mopping the kitchen floor after breakfast, I hear Anna and Dressie laughing and bursting with excitement. I wish I knew what has made them so happy. It's not like Lady Helena doesn't go out to the local bar every Saturday night and doesn't come home until late the next day, so they can't be excited about that. They have something up their sleeve, and it better not be a house party. I will be stuck cleaning the house by myself if they refuse to help me. Though I will give it to my sisters, they usually do their best to clean up as quickly and as efficiently as possible before she returns.

I hear echoes of Lady Helena's conversation with Anna and Dressie, so I rush and hide in the shadowed alcove under the stairs. I am drawn to the commotion like a moth to a flame, my curiosity piqued by the animated voices that echo from the dining room. Little did I know that what awaited me would unravel the fragile threads of hope that I had clung to so desperately.

As I stand, concealed from view yet privy to the clandestine discourse unfolding before me, the words spoken by Lady Helena cut through the air like a blade. She speaks of a Royal Play Party and of the opportunity it presents for Anna and Dressie to woo the prince and for one of them to secure her place by his side as his future wife.

The realization lands upon me like a blow to the chest, stealing the breath from my lungs and leaving me reeling in its wake. The prince, a figure of mystery and allure, has long been the subject of whispered fantasies among the young women of Sapphire City. And now, it seems, Lady Helena has seized the opportunity to keep my fantasies about meeting the prince from coming true. She is hiding my invitation so that I can't even get into the palace if I could come up with a dress to wear.

I listen to the conversation that unfolds between them. Their voices, filled with excitement and anticipation, ring out like a cruel mockery of the dreams that I dare to harbor within my heart.

"Imagine, Anna, being the future queen of Sapphire City," Lady Helena exclaims, her voice dripping with pride and ambition. "With the prince at your side, you would be the envy of all who behold you, and we would never have to worry about money again."

Anna, ever eager to please, responds with a fervor that borders on desperation. "Oh, Mother, it would be a dream come true! To be the wife of the prince, to rule by his side. It is all I have ever wanted."

Dressie, her voice a symphony of gleeful anticipation, chimes in with her own aspirations. "And imagine the parties, the balls, the endless nights of revelry. To be the belle of the court, adored by all who lay eyes upon you. It is a fate beyond compare. A fate, dear sister, that I do hope I get to have! But no matter which one of us catches the prince's eye, I know that the other will be happy."

"Agreed, Sister," Anna says to Dressie.

Their words, filled with ambition and longing, serve as a stark reminder of the divide that separates us. While they dream of a future filled with splendor and adoration, I am left to grapple with the harsh reality of my station in life, a life dictated by duty and obligation rather than desire.

As the conversation fades into the distance, I am left alone with the weight of my sadness, the hollow ache of unfulfilled dreams gnawing at the edges of my soul. The prince, a distant figure shrouded in mystery, remains forever beyond my reach, a tantalizing mirage on the horizon of my existence, forever out of grasp.

And so, with a heavy heart and tear-stained eyes, I retreat into the solitude of my thoughts, the echoes of Lady Helena's conversation haunting me like a ghost of what could have been. I head up the stairs and into my room. I am just a forgotten soul adrift in a sea of unattainable dreams.

Dressie

As we watch our mother's retreating figure disappear into the afternoon, a mixture of relief and anticipation washes over us. This is our chance to finally reveal the truth to Isabella and to right the wrongs that have plagued her for far too long. First, we go into mom's room and turn it upside down until we find Izzy's invitation.

"Izzy, can we talk to you?" Anna's voice quivers with a mixture of apprehension and determination as she steps forward.

My heart races with nervous energy as I join my sister, echoing her sentiment. "Yeah, we need to tell you something important."

Izzy turns to face us, her eyes wide with curiosity and uncertainty. "What's going on, Anna, Dressie? What's this about?"

Taking a deep breath, I summon the courage to speak. "It's about the Royal Play Party. We...we need to talk to you about it and give you something."

Anna nods in agreement, her voice steady as she continues, "We know our mother hid your invitation, and we would have come to you sooner with it, but we had no idea what she had done with it until Dressie saw her reading it in her bedroom earlier today. So, we just went into her room and found it for you. We couldn't let her keep you from going. You know how much we love you and want the best for you. You know that we don't share her feelings for you. We want you to have your chance to meet the prince, and if you are the one who catches his eye, we will be happy for you."

I watch as relief floods Isabella's features, her eyes shining with gratitude and disbelief. Tears glisten in her eyes as she whispers her thanks, her voice barely audible over the pounding of my heart.

Anna steps forward, her own eyes brimming with emotion, "We may not have an extra dress for you, but we'll figure something out. We want all three of us to have the most amazing night."

Together, the three of us stand in the dimly lit corridor, bound by a shared sense of purpose and determination. This is our chance to show Isabella that she is not alone, that she is loved and valued by us, her sisters.

And so, with renewed resolve, we begin to make plans for the Royal Play Party, a night that promises to be a celebration of sisterhood, solidarity, and the unbreakable bond that ties us together.

Chapter Five

Isabella

Despite Anna and Dressie's best efforts, we couldn't figure out how to get me a dress and shoes for the Royal Play Party, and the realization was crushing. I told them to go ahead and get ready and that I would be alright. Now, as I lay across my bed, tears streaming down my cheeks, I feel the weight of despair pressing down upon me like a suffocating blanket.

I had dared to hope, dared to dream of a night filled with laughter and joy, only to have those hopes dashed against the jagged rocks of reality. How could I possibly attend such a prestigious event without the proper attire? I am a mere shadow among the glittering lights of Sapphire City, invisible and insignificant in the eyes of those who hold power and privilege.

Just when I feel as though I cannot bear the weight of my despair any longer, a soft knock sounds at my door, pulling me from the depths of my sorrow. With a heavy sigh, I rise from my bed and shuffle towards the door, steeling myself for another blow to my already battered spirit.

To my astonishment, standing on the threshold is none other than my godmother, Elizabeth. It has been years since I last saw her, since the tragic day my father passed away, and her presence fills me with a sense of both comfort and confusion.

"Isabella, darling, may I come in?" Elizabeth's voice is warm and soothing, a balm to my fractured soul.

I nod wordlessly, too stunned to form coherent thoughts and step aside to allow her entry. As she crosses the threshold, I cannot believe that she is here.

"I haven't seen you in years since Dad passed. What are you doing here?" I ask.

"You know your stepmother, and I don't get along, and she would blow a gasket now if she knew that I was here. But I should have found a way to keep in touch. I am sorry," she says as she holds in her arms a dress bag, another small bag, and a shoe box.

"How...how did you know I needed a dress?" I stammer, my mind reeling with disbelief.

Elizabeth offers me a reassuring smile, her eyes twinkling with mischief. "Oh, my dear, a godmother always knows when her goddaughter is in need. And when I heard that you were in need of a dress for the Royal Play Party, I simply couldn't resist coming to your rescue."

I bust out in laughter, and she says, "Okay, okay! Anna called me! But that sounded good, didn't it!"

I am overwhelmed by her generosity and by the lengths she has gone to ensure that I have the opportunity to attend the event that means so much to me.

"Okay, let's get you dressed, and then I will get all you girls' hair and makeup done," she says.

She hands me the small bag first.

I open the bags and pull out a lace garter set, and I look at her with confusion as I crease my eyebrows.

"What's this for?" I ask, my voice tinged with uncertainty.

Elizabeth's smile widens, a knowing glint in her eyes. "Consider it a little something to spice up your evening, my dear. You never know when you might meet someone special and want to have a bit of fun."

Despite my initial reservations, I find myself unable to resist the infectious enthusiasm in Elizabeth's voice. With a sense of newfound determination, I accept the garter set and allow her to guide me through the process of getting ready for the party.

Together, we transform my bedroom into a makeshift dressing room, laughter and chatter filling the air as Elizabeth helps me slip into the sleek purple dress and towering straps of high heels. With each passing moment, I feel myself shedding the cloak of despair that has weighed me down, replaced by a sense of excitement and anticipation for the evening ahead.

The dress hugs my curves in all the right places, and the heels exude confidence and allure.

As I stand before the mirror, my reflection staring back at me with a newfound confidence, I realize that tonight is not just about attending a party. It's about reclaiming my sense of self, about embracing the woman I am meant to be.

Beside me, my sisters Anna and Dressie buzz with excitement, their laughter filling the room as they flit about like butterflies, their eyes sparkling with anticipation. And then, there is Elizabeth, who may be my godmother, but she has always been there for the three of us, no matter what.

She stands before us now, a vision of elegance and grace, her hands deftly working their magic as she expertly applies makeup and arranges our hair in intricate styles. With each stroke of her brush, each twist of her fingers, she transforms us into the epitome of beauty and glamour, ready to take on the world.

As she works, we share stories, memories, hopes, and dreams. We speak of the future that lies before us, of the challenges and adventures that await. And amidst the laughter and chatter, there is a sense of camaraderie, of sisterhood, a bond that transcends time and space.

"So, Isabella," Elizabeth says, her voice soft and gentle as she applies a final coat of lipstick, "are you excited for tonight?"

I nod eagerly, a smile tugging at the corners of my lips. "Yes, I am," I reply, my heart racing with anticipation. "I can't wait to see what the night has in store for us."

Anna and Dressie chime in, their voices filled with excitement as they share their own thoughts and feelings.

"I know I am excited. I haven't been to a play party in months!" Dressie says.

"I know you are extremely excited!" Elizabeth says to Dressie.

"Wait, is there something different about this party that I need to know?" I ask them.

Elizabeth and Dressie laugh, and Anna just shakes her head.

"Nothing that you need to know right now," Elizabeth says as she continues to do my hair.

Finally, we are all ready to go. We stand there together, united in our anticipation; I know that no matter what the night may bring, we will face it together as sisters, as friends, as allies in a world that is both beautiful and uncertain.

With a final glance in the mirror, we take each other's hands and step out into the night. And as we make our way to the palace, I feel a sense of exhilaration wash over me.

Chapter Six

Isabella

Lady Helena had ordered a limousine for Anna and Dressie. It pulled up at our house at exactly 6:30 p.m. We were all standing in the window, watching for it with so much excitement. I stand here thinking about Lady Helena and how she may be my evil stepmother, but Anna and Dressie are more than my stepsisters; they are my real family, and I love them. We have a bond that was built before my father died and that continued to grow after behind Lady Helena's back.

As we walk to the limo, the driver has gotten out and is opening the door for us.

"Good evening, ladies. You all look beautiful tonight. Sit back and enjoy your ride to the palace. There is Champagne cooling in ice and glasses ready for you," he says to us as we get inside.

Before he shuts the door, we all say, "Thank you".

As we approach the palace, the anticipation bubbles within me like a tempestuous sea, threatening to engulf me in its swirling currents of excitement and trepidation. The night air crackles with an electric energy, a palpable sense of anticipation hanging thick in the air like a heavy fog.

The palace looms before us, its towering spires reaching towards the heavens like the outstretched fingers of a benevolent deity. The glow of torches and lanterns casts a warm, inviting light upon the throngs of guests gathering outside, their voices rising in a cacophonous symphony of laughter and chatter.

As we make our way, with the rest of the crowd, towards the imposing figures of the palace's guards and one servant standing sentinel at the entrance, their stoic expressions betray nothing of the tumultuous emotions swirling within me. With each step forward, my heart pounds in my chest, the anticipation of what awaits us within the palace walls threatening to consume me whole.

We enter the grand ballroom, and I am immediately struck by the sheer opulence of our surroundings. The room is bathed in a soft, golden light, the flickering flames of countless candles casting dancing shadows upon the walls. The air is alive with the hum of conversation and the strains of music drifting from somewhere unseen.

But as my eyes sweep across the room, taking in the grandeur of our surroundings, they come to rest upon a sight that leaves me reeling with shock and disbelief.

The ballroom, that I can only imagine was a bastion of elegance and refinement, has been transformed into some sort of massive bedroom with all sorts of things that I have no idea what they are or what they are used for, but the room looks like torture chamber like what you would expect the dungeon to look like but with massive beds. My breath catches in my throat as I take in the scene before me—the beds lining the walls, adorned with satin sheets and plush pillows, the array of furniture and, oh my god, I know what those are, sex toys laid out upon tables scattered throughout the room, the dance floor in the center of the room pulsating with the rhythmic movements of couples engaged in their own private dances of desire.

Anna and Dressie stand beside me, their expressions a mirror of my own shock and disbelief. But beneath the surface, I sense a spark of intrigue, a curiosity that threatens to overcome their initial reservations.

"I can't believe this," Dressie whispers over the din of the crowd. "It's...it's like something out of a dream. This is literally a BDSM play party! I have been to several in England. Anna, you remember me telling you about them, about the lifestyle, about the fun of dominance and submission?"

Anna nods her head, her eyes wide with wonder. "Yes, I remember your stories, and this is better than I ever imagined. I've never seen anything like it. It's...it's so...liberating and exciting."

Their words echo in my ears, stirring something deep within me. A mixture of curiosity and apprehension that threatens to pull me in opposite directions. But as I look around at the sea of faces, each one a testament to the diversity of desires that converge within these hallowed halls, I feel a sense of intrigue washes over me.

"I don't understand. Dressie, you never mentioned anything like this to me. Why not?" I ask.

"It wasn't that I didn't want to tell you. It is just because you are so...so innocent. I think that's a good word. I didn't think you would understand my sexual desires and how I enjoy living the lifestyle when I can. I knew the invitation said, "play party" I thought maybe it was a real play party, but then I thought, it's the prince of Sapphire City; he wouldn't be into BDSM," Dressie says.

"You will tell me EVERYTHING later! But you may be right. Just one question, how did you hear about this world?" I ask.

"Who do you think took me to my first party? Elizabeth!" Dressie replies, laughing.

My mouth falls open; I look between Dressie and Anna, shaking my head. "Wow, I had no idea. I am not sure I should be here."

"Well, you are here now, and you are not leaving. Dressie may understand and be a part of this world, but I am not. So, you will not leave me. I want to know more. From her stories, I have wanted to know more and to decide if this was a world that I want to be a part of," Anna says to me.

"Fine. I will stay for a while," I reply.

And so, with a sense of nervousness, intrigue, and sisterhood, I decide to stay. I follow them further into the room trying not to look how I felt that I didn't belong. I caught my mouth hanging open in surprise several times, praying that no one saw me.

A few moments later, he approaches me. The prince has approached me! I can't breathe.

Chapter Seven

Prince James

I STAND ON THE balcony, watching the guests come in and cross the threshold. I see the most beautiful woman walk through the door. Amidst the swirling throng of guests, my gaze is drawn inexorably towards her. She is a vision of beauty amidst the sea of faces, her presence casting a spell upon me that I cannot hope to resist.

I want to meet her. It was like my body was moving towards her on its own. I have no control. I see her standing in conversation with the two women she walked in with. With every step closer, my heart pounds in my chest with a rhythm that matches the tempo of the music echoing through the grand ballroom. Every move brings me closer to her, to the enigmatic woman who has captured my attention with nothing more than a single glance.

Approaching her, I am struck by her beauty. Her eyes are pools of liquid fire that seem to hold the secrets of the universe within their depths; her lips, full and inviting, curved into a smile that sets my heart ablaze with desire.

"May I have this dance?" I ask, my voice filled with a quiet intensity.

Her response is a soft gasp, a flutter of lashes against porcelain cheeks as she meets my gaze with a mixture of surprise and uncertainty. Yet, beneath the surface, I sense a spark of something deeper. A longing, perhaps, or a desire that mirrors my own.

"Um...I would love to, your Highness," she says.

I take her hand and lead her to the dance floor.

As we move across the dance floor, our bodies swaying in time with the music, I am struck by the way she feels in my arms, the warmth of her skin, the delicate curve of her waist, and the way she shivers beneath my touch. It is a sensation unlike any I have ever experienced, a connection that transcends the boundaries of the physical realm.

In her eyes, I see a glimpse of something primal, something raw and untamed, an echo of the submissive nature that lies dormant within her soul. But it is more than that. It is a spark of defiance, a flicker of strength that sets her apart from the others.

"What are your dreams and desires?" I ask softly, my voice a whisper against the swell of music.

Her response is hesitant, guarded, "I don't know how to answer that question. I have a feeling what I say will not be the type of dreams and desires that you are referring to."

In that moment, I take her hand in mine, my grip firm yet gentle as I lead her away from the pulsating throng of dancers. We walk in silence, the weight of unspoken words hanging heavy between us, until, at last, we find ourselves alone in a secluded alcove.

"Come with me," I whisper, my voice barely audible over the thrum of our hearts beating in unison. "Let me show you a world beyond the confines of convention, a world where pleasure and pain intertwine in a delicate dance of submission and dominance."

Hesitantly, with her eyes wide with fear and uncertainty, she lets me take her on a path that I am hoping will lead her to face the desires that I saw in her eyes when she walked in tonight. I can feel the weight of responsibility settle upon my shoulders. Tonight, I will introduce her to a world unlike any she has ever known, a world of pleasure and pain, of trust and surrender.

As I lead her through the crowded room, I can feel the tension crackling in the air like electricity. The scent of arousal hangs heavy around us, mingling with the soft strains of music and the murmurs of conversation that fill the room.

"Watch closely, Isabella," I murmur, my voice low as I guide her towards a raised platform at the center of the room. "This is where the real magic happens."

As we approach, I can see the scene unfolding before us. A Dom and his sub are locked in a dance of desire and submission. The Dom stands tall and imposing, his presence commanding the attention of everyone in the room. His sub kneels before him, her eyes downcast, her body a canvas upon which he will paint his desires.

"See how he controls her with just a word, a touch," I say, my voice barely above a whisper as I point out the subtle cues that pass between them. "He is her Master, her guide in this world of pleasure and pain."

As the scene unfolds, I watch Isabella closely, taking note of the way her eyes widen with curiosity and intrigue. I can see the questions swirling in her mind, the desire to understand this world that is so foreign to her.

"And now, watch as he begins to play," I continue, my voice filled with anticipation as the Dom selects a flogger from the nearby rack. "See how he uses the tools at his disposal to bring her pleasure, to push her boundaries and explore the depths of her desires."

As the first strike lands, I watch as she flinches, her eyes widening with surprise. But as the scene progresses, I can also see something else, a flicker of arousal, a spark of excitement that ignites within her.

"It's okay to feel conflicted, Isabella," I say, my voice gentle yet firm as I take her hand in mine. "This world is not black and white. It is filled with shades of gray. But remember, you are always in control. You have the power to explore this world at your own pace, to decide what feels right for you." In that moment, I realize that she is more than just a passing fancy; she is a puzzle, a mystery waiting to be unraveled, a challenge that I am determined to conquer.

She removes her hand from mine, turns to look at me, and with a whispered apology, she turns and flees from the party, leaving me standing alone in the dimly lit corridor, my heart heavy with regret and longing.

I stand there for a split second before running after her. I reach the palace steps that lead out to the doors, but I don't see her anywhere. It is like she vanished into the thin air. Like I had been in a dream for the last two hours.

As the moon hangs high in the night sky, casting its silver glow upon the sprawling grounds of the palace, I find myself consumed by a singular purpose, a relentless determination to find the mysterious woman who has captured my attention. With every step I take, the urgency of my pursuit weighs heavily upon me, driving me forward with a fervor born of desire and longing.

The memory of her haunts me; her image burned into my mind like a brand upon my soul. Her beauty, ethereal and otherworldly, has left an indelible mark upon my heart, igniting a fire within me that refuses to be quenched. I cannot rest until I find her until I unravel the mystery of her identity and claim her as my own.

But as I press on in my pursuit, I find myself interrupted and distracted by a woman who is persistent in diverting my attention to her and her insistent pleas for my favor. Her presence is a thorn in my side. I fend off her advances, and that's when I see it, a small, delicate ribbon fluttering in the breeze like a silent sentinel on the palace steps. In its simplicity, it becomes a symbol of the connection that binds me to the mysterious woman, a tangible reminder of the fleeting encounter that has left me longing for more.

With renewed determination, I scoop up the ribbon, clutching it tightly in my hand. Tomorrow, I will send out the Royal Guard to find the lady who has captured my heart.

CHAPTER EIGHT

THE NEXT DAY DAWNS bright and clear, but my thoughts are consumed by thoughts of her. With a sense of purpose that borders on obsession, I rally the Royal Guards and send them out in a widespread effort to identify and locate her.

With determination etched upon my face, I charge through the palace grounds, my footsteps echoing loudly across the concrete path. My urgency is palpable, a tangible force that propels me forward with a single-minded determination that brooks no opposition.

I tell the Royal Guards to scour every corner of the kingdom, follow every lead, and pursue every possible avenue of inquiry. And though it may seem like finding a needle in a haystack, I am undeterred in my quest to find her. I will reunite with the mysterious woman who has captured my heart and claim her as my own.

The Head of the Royal Guard

As the Head of the Royal Guards, it is my duty to ensure the safety and security of the palace and its inhabitants. But on this particular night, as Prince James sets off in pursuit of the mysterious woman who has captured his attention, I find myself faced with a challenge unlike any I have encountered before.

It is obvious by his pacing around the palace that his thoughts are consumed by thoughts of the mysterious woman who has captured his attention. With a sense of determination that borders on obsession, he rallies the Royal Guards to go out and check every corner of the kingdom and to not stop until we find this woman.

I am tasked with leading the search. It is a daunting challenge that tests the limits of our ingenuity and perseverance. But despite the obstacles that stand in our way, we press on, driven by the knowledge that the prince's happiness hangs in the balance.

We searched for two days with no avail. I swear if I have to talk to any more women trying their best to lie that it was them, I am going to blow up. As I stand in front of this modest home and knock on the door, I hope that this is the house of the woman I am looking for.

Anna & Dressie

The knock comes to the door, one that Dressie and I have been expecting. We had heard that the Royal Guards had been scouring around the kingdom looking for a woman who owned a dress that matched some ribbon that the prince found after the woman ran off at the Royal Play Party.

For the life of me, I cannot imagine what woman in her right mind would have run away from the prince.

As Dressie and I stand before the Head of the Royal Guard and our mother, her imperious gaze bearing down upon us with a weight that threatens to crush my resolve, I feel a bead of sweat trickling down the back of my neck. My sister Dressie stands beside me, her expression a mirror of my own. We are trying hard to hide the fact that Izzy came to the party with us. It was as if our mother could read our minds and knew that we were hiding something. But we also knew that the ribbon the guard was holding belonged to Izzy, and we wanted the guard to know that. We wanted the prince to take her away from our mother's grip and be treated better.

"We think we know what you are looking for," I told the guard. Izzy is cleaning the kitchen while all of this is going on. "Follow us to the attic."

"Anna, Dressie, what is the meaning of this?" Lady Helena's voice is sharp, cutting through the air like a knife as she fixes us with a stern glare.

I exchange a nervous glance with Dressie, swallowing hard as I steel myself for what is to come. "Mother, you will see," I begin, my voice trembling with uncertainty. "The dress he is looking for is in the attic."

Lady Helena's eyes narrow, suspicion flickering behind their icy facade. "What about the dress? Speak, child, and do not keep me waiting."

But neither of us speak. We walk to the attic and open the door and let the guard inside. The dress is hanging in a garnet bag. I walk over and unzip it for the guard. When I turn, my mother's face was beat red with anger.

The guard says, "That's it! It is an exact match! Which one of you does the dress belong to?"

I take a deep breath, gathering my courage as I prepare to reveal the truth. "The dress...the dress belongs to...to our other sister, Isabella," I confess, the words tumbling from my lips in a rush of desperation. "She...she put it here in the attic after the party."

For a moment, there is silence, a heavy, oppressive silence that hangs in the air like a shroud, suffocating in its intensity. Mother's expression darkens, her features twisted into a mask of rage as she turns her steely gaze upon us.

"Isabella," she snarls, the name dripping from her lips like venom. "She couldn't have gone to the party." Then she turns to the guard and says, "I believe my daughters are mistaken and that it belongs to one of them."

"I would have to believe that if it did belong to one of them, that they would speak up. I want to talk to your other daughter," the guard states.

"She's not my, she's not my daughter!" Mother yells and stomps out of the attic. We all follow her. Under her breath, she says, "I will deal with Isabella later."

The Head of the Royal Guard

As the Head of the Royal Guard, it falls upon me to ensure that all matters are handled with the utmost efficiency and diligence. With Lady Helena's refusal to cooperate in bringing Isabella to try on the dress, I know that I must take matters into my own hands.

"Lady Helena," I begin, my voice firm and unwavering as I address her, "you will go and fetch Isabella so that she may try on the dress. I will accompany you downstairs to ensure that you comply."

But Lady Helena's response is immediate, her defiance palpable in the air as she squares her shoulders and meets my gaze head-on. "I will not do it," she declares, her voice laced with stubborn resolve. "I refuse to be a part of this charade."

I feel a surge of frustration coursing through me at her obstinance, knowing that time is of the essence in resolving this matter. "Lady Helena," I say, my tone sharp with authority, "you leave me no choice. If you do not comply, I will have no option but to place you under arrest for obstruction of royal business against the orders of the prince."

For a moment, it seems as though Lady Helena will continue to resist, her features contorted with anger and indignation. But ultimately, the weight of my words proves too much to bear, and with a reluctant sigh, she begrudgingly acquiesces.

As we make our way downstairs, I can feel the tension in the air thickening with each step. Lady Helena snarls at Isabella, who looks scared. *This poor girl, I don't know what is going on in this house, but if she isn't the woman the prince is looking for, I want to come back and make sure she is okay.*

When Isabella emerges from upstairs wearing the dress, there is no mistaking the look of recognition that passes over my features. It is her, the mysterious woman who captured the prince's attention at the Royal Play Party.

Without hesitation, I reach for my phone and dial Prince James' number, knowing that he needs to be informed immediately that we have found her.

Prince James

As I stand in my father's office, my heart pounding with anticipation, I await the call from the Royal Guard with bated breath. The search for the woman whose ribbon I found has consumed my thoughts, driving me to the brink of desperation. And then, finally, the phone rings, a sharp, insistent sound that cuts through the silence like a knife.

I snatch up the receiver, my hand trembling with excitement as I bring it to my ear. "Your Highness," the voice of the Head of the Guard crackles over the line, his words urgent and clipped. "We've found her. She is one of the daughters of Lady Helena. Her name is Isabella."

A surge of exhilaration courses through me at the news, my heart pounding with anticipation. Without hesitation, I tell the Guard, "That is wonderful news. I want to speak with her. Pass her the phone." My voice cracks with a mixture of hope and longing as I await her response.

And then, finally, her voice fills the line. A soft, melodic sound that sends a shiver of excitement coursing through me.

"Prince James," she says, her tone hesitant and somewhat scared.

"Good afternoon, Isabella. My Royal Guard informed me that the ribbon belongs to your dress. We need to talk in person. I have so many questions about why you left that night; did you feel the chemistry between you and me, like I did; and more," I tell her. I wanted to say more. More about her becoming my princess, but I didn't want to scare her off. I need to get her to the palace to talk to me in person. "Just come back with the Guards, and let's sit down and talk. I want to give you a proposition."

"I understand that you have questions Sire, and that you want to talk, but I need time to think. There is a lot about your world that I don't fully understand, and I need to think about how this affects me. I will consider coming to the palace to discuss any questions and propositions you may have, but I cannot give you an answer right now. Give me an hour to get my thoughts together."

Her words hang in the air like a delicate thread, fragile yet full of promise. And though a part of me longs to plead with her, to beg her to give me an answer then and there, I know that I must respect her wishes and give her the time and space she needs to make such an important decision.

"I understand, Isabella," I reply, my voice tinged with disappointment yet filled with understanding. "Take all the time you need. But know that I will be waiting for you whenever you are ready."

As I hang up the phone, my mind races with a thousand thoughts and emotions. Hope and fear war within me, uncertainty gnawing at the edges of my resolve. But amidst the tumult, one thing remains clear, I will wait for Isabella for her to come to the palace and talk to me. I know that she will at least give me that, and once she is here, I can talk her into being my wife and my sub. I can show her what her life will be like. I can show her what I felt radiating off of her at the party; she is a natural sub, and her sexual desires are more than what she lets on.

CHAPTER NINE

Isabella

I HAVE FINISHED WASHING the lunch dishes and I am starting to sweep the kitchen floor when I hear all the commotion of loud voices and footsteps coming from upstairs. I knew by the tone of Lady Helena's voice that she is angry and that always means that she is coming to yell at me for something.

I continue to sweep until Lady Helena, Anna, Dressie, and a man from the Royal Guard walk into the kitchen. *The Royal Guard. What are they doing here?*

"Izzy," Anna speaks first. "The head of the Royal Guard is here today looking for the dress that belongs to this ribbon."

I stop sweeping and look up. The man from the Royal Guard has my ribbon that I wore around my neck, made from the fabric of the dress Elizabeth bought me, in his hand.

I look between Anna and Dressie. They are smiling from ear to ear. Then I look at Lady Helena and if looks could kill, I would be dead. Her eyes are pure red and evil, but she doesn't say a word.

The man looks at Lady Helena. When she doesn't say anything, he holds the ribbon out to me and says, "Your sisters recognized the ribbon and led me to the dress upstairs in the attic that it belongs to. They say that the dress belongs to you. I need you to go put on the dress so that I may verify that the dress fits you."

Dressie comes over, takes the broom, and leans it against the counter. Then she takes my hand and says, "Come on, Izzy. Anna and I will help you put on the dress."

I didn't say anything, nor did I look back at Lady Helena. I let Dressie lead me to the attic with Anna walking behind us.

When we get to the attic, and Anna shuts the door, I say to both of them, "Why did you tell him that the dress is mine? You know Lady Helena is going to make my life so much worse now."

Anna grabs my hand and says, "This is your chance, Izzy. You know Dressie and I love you and blood could never have made you more of our sister than you are. We want the best for you and this is your way out of here. Your way out from the grasps of our mother. A chance for you to have a better life. A life you deserve."

"I know our bond as sisters can never be stronger than it already is, but me a princess with a prince whose lifestyle is one I don't understand and one that I am not sure if I want to. Getting away from Lady Helena sounds great, but at what cost?" I ask.

"I promise you little sister, that once you understand the lifestyle better, you may see that it is not as bad as you imagine it to be. I can say this, it will build a bond between you and the prince much stronger than just being his princess and wife. And Anna and I are always here for you," Dressie replies.

They help me into the dress, and we walk downstairs to the den where Lady Helena and the Guard are. Lady Helena lets out a nasty noise, but the Guard smiles and says, "Beautiful. I will call Prince James."

He takes out his cell phone and tells the prince that he has found me. Then he hands me the phone.

As I hold the phone to my ear, Prince James' words echo through the receiver, filling me with a whirlwind of emotions. His proposal hangs in the air, a weighty silence stretching across the distance as I grapple with the enormity of his offer. The societal expectations that have shaped my life loom large in my mind, urging caution and restraint, while the allure of the prince's proposition beckons me toward a future unknown.

"Isabella," he says, his voice gentle yet insistent, "I need your answer. Will you come to the castle to discuss my proposition?"

I pause, my heart pounding in my chest as I weigh my options. The thought of defying convention and embracing a future filled with uncertainty fills me with both excitement and fear. But before I can respond, I know that I need time to think, to consider the implications of my decision and what it may mean for my future.

"Prince James," I say, my voice steady despite the turmoil raging within me, "I appreciate your offer, but I need time to think. I will let your guard know if I will come to the castle to discuss any proposition you may have, but I cannot give you an answer right now. Just give me a few hours to think about it."

There is a moment of silence on the other end of the line, the weight of his disappointment palpable even through the distance of the phone. But as I listen to the steady rhythm of his breathing, I know that he understands. The gravity of the decision before me is not one to be made lightly, and he respects my need for time to consider my options.

"Of course, Isabella," he finally replies, his voice tinged with understanding. "Take all the time you need. But know that I will be waiting for you whenever you are ready."

With a sense of relief flooding through me, I bid him farewell and lower the phone from my ear, the weight of his words lingering in the air around me. I hand the phone back to the guard and he tells me that he will be outside waiting for me. When I am ready, just come outside.

"You don't have to wait. I don't know how long it will take for me to decide," I say.

He walks closer and says so Lady Helena doesn't hear him, "I can tell there is something wrong here with your stepmom. I am not leaving here without you. So, take as long as you need to. I will be outside."

"Come on, Izzy," Dressie says, grabbing my hand. "Let's go to our room."

Dressie, Anna, and I went upstairs to their room. Anna shuts the door behind us, locks it, and says, "Let's talk."

As we gather on the bed like we are still little girls, the weight of recent events hangs heavy in the air, casting a somber pall over our conversation. I can feel their curious gazes upon me, their eyes brimming with unspoken questions, as they wait for me to share my side of the story.

"Isabella," Anna begins, her voice soft and tentative. "We've been wanting to ask you...about the Royal Play Party and what you thought, but now we need to know what happened there? How did you meet the prince?"

I take a deep breath, gathering my thoughts as I prepare to recount the events of that fateful night. "It all happened so quickly," I admit, my voice tinged with a hint of uncertainty. "I was there with you both, enjoying the festivities, when suddenly, he appeared before me. Prince James."

Dressie nods in understanding, her expression a mixture of curiosity and intrigue. "And then what happened?" she prompts, her eyes alight with interest.

"He asked me to dance," as I continue, my mind drifting back to the memory of his strong arms around me, the warmth of his touch sending shivers down my spine. "And as we danced, he...he spoke to me. Asked me about my dreams, my d esires..."

Anna's brow furrows in confusion, her gaze searching mine for answers. "And what did you tell him?" she inquires, her voice filled with genuine curiosity.

I pause for a moment, considering my response carefully. "I told him the truth," I reply, my voice steady despite the uncertainty that lingers within me. "That no matter how I answered that question, it wouldn't be the answer to the question the way that he meant it. So, he took my hand and walked me to a scene in the middle of the room. I watched, and he talked me through some of what was going on. Then I ran out and came home."

There is a moment of silence as my words hang in the air, the weight of them settling over us like a heavy cloak. Then, Dressie speaks up, her voice soft but determined. "Isabella, what do you think about...about BDSM?"

The question catches me off guard, and for a moment, I struggle to find the right words to express myself. "I...I don't know," I admit, my voice barely above a whisper. "It's all so new to me, so...foreign. But there's something about it that intrigues me, that...that draws me in."

As I speak, I can feel the weight of their gazes upon me, their silent support and understanding comforting me in ways I cannot fully articulate. In this moment, surrounded by my sisters, I know that no matter what lies ahead, I will not face it alone. And with their unwavering love and support by my side, I am ready to embark on this journey of self-discovery, no matter where it may lead.

"Well, that's good news! I, for one, can say that I am happy that both of my sisters share my sexual fetishes!" Dressie says, giving out a loud breath.

Anna laughs and says, "You and I are in the same boat Izzy. We both have never experienced BDSM, but we are both intrigued. We can talk our way through our feelings together with Dressie being a force of knowledge. But you, you will also have the prince. You really need to go with the guard. This is your way out of here, your way out from under our mother."

I look at Dressie, and she says, "Please go. Take this opportunity to get out of here, have the life you have always deserved, and experience something new. Let the prince show you a new life. We are going to be here for you every step of the way, because you can't leave and us not come visit!"

With tears in my eyes, I say, "Thank you both for always loving me and being here for me. You are going to have to come stay at the palace some and visit me every day. I can't do this without you two."

We all sit on the bed a few more minutes in a bear hug before we get up, and they come to the attic and help me pack the few things that I owned, making sure that I took all of my memories of my parents with me.

The three of us carry my stuff out to the car and pass Lady Helena, who literally growls at us. The guard grabs my things and puts them in the trunk. I give my sisters another big hug before getting in the back of the Rolls Royce and start to drive away. I sit there looking back at the house that I grew up in, the house that held all the memories of both my parents that had become overshadowed by the hatefulness of Lady Helena. My emotions were a mixture of relief and fear. Fear of the unknown. Fear of what the prince expects of me and fear that I won't be who he thinks I am or what he wants me to be, and he will send me right back into hell.

CHAPTER TEN

Prince James

As Isabella arrives at the palace, I can't help but feel a surge of anticipation coursing through me. I've been eagerly awaiting this moment, eager to spend more time with her and delve deeper into the connection that has sparked between us.

As she steps through the grand entrance, her presence commands attention, her grace and poise captivating me in an instant. I take a moment to admire her, noting the way her eyes light up with curiosity as she takes in her surroundings.

"Welcome to the palace," I say, my voice warm as I extend a hand towards her. "I'm glad you could join me."

Her smile is genuine, her eyes sparkling with excitement as she takes my hand in hers. "Thank you for having me," she replies, her voice soft but filled with warmth.

As we begin our tour of the palace, I can't help but notice the way her eyes widen in awe at the opulence that surrounds her. I lead her through the grand corridors, pointing out various points of interest and sharing stories of the palace's history.

But it's when we reach my private quarters that her curiosity truly peaks. As I open the door and we step inside, I can see she is relieved that it is not my playroom. But I walk over, open the closet door, and usher her inside. "I know what you were expecting to see in my bedroom, but it is hidden from my parents. It is through here. I had it built while they were traveling around the country a year ago."

When she steps into the closet, I hit a secret button on the wall behind my shirts, and we walk in. Her eyes widen in surprise, her gaze taking in the array of BDSM toys and equipment that adorn the room.

"I know this may seem...unconventional," I begin, my voice tinged with uncertainty. "But for me, BDSM is about trust, about exploration, about pushing boundaries and discovering new depths of pleasure."

I watch her closely, gauging her reaction as she takes in my words. To my relief, her expression is one of intrigue rather than judgment, her eyes alight with curiosity as she takes in her surroundings.

"I've always been drawn to the power dynamics inherent in BDSM," I continue, my voice growing more confident as I speak. "For me, it's about more than just physical pleasure. It's about connection, about trust, about surrendering to the moment and allowing yourself to be vulnerable."

As I speak, I can see a flicker of understanding in her eyes, a recognition of the deeper meaning behind my words. And in that moment, I know that she sees me for who I truly am, a man driven by passion, by desire, and by a longing for connection that transcends the physical.

Together, we explore the depths of my playroom, discussing our shared interests and desires with a newfound sense of openness and honesty. And as the hours slip away, I find myself growing increasingly captivated by the woman before me, her strength, her courage, and her unwavering curiosity igniting a fire within me that refuses to be extinguished.

In her presence, I feel alive in a way I haven't in years, my heart pounding with anticipation as we continue to delve deeper into the unknown. And as we stand together in the heart of my playroom, surrounded by the trappings of our shared desires,

I know that this is only the beginning of a journey that promises to be as exhilarating as it is transformative.

We leave my room and head down to the sitting room where my parents are. We walk into the room, and as I stand before my parents, Isabella by my side, I cannot shake the feeling of unease that gnaws at the pit of my stomach. Their eyes linger upon her, a curious glint of recognition sparking within their depths, and for a moment, the air hangs heavy with unspoken questions.

"There is something familiar about you, my dear," my mother says, her voice filled with warmth and affection. "Have we met before?"

Isabella hesitates, her gaze flickering between my parents and me, before finally gathering her courage and speaking. "Yes," she says, her voice barely above a whisper. "I am Isabella Tremaine."

The revelation hangs in the air like a heavy cloud, casting a pall over the room as my parents exchange a look of shock and disbelief. For a moment, I am frozen in place, unable to comprehend the implications of her words, unable to reconcile the image of the woman before me with the memories of the girl I once knew.

But as the truth sinks in, a wave of conflicting emotions washes over me. There is a tidal wave of shock, anger, and betrayal that threatens to consume me whole. How could she keep such a secret from me? How could she deceive me into believing that she was someone else entirely?

As I struggle to come to terms with the truth, I see the hurt and confusion reflected in Isabella's eyes, a mirror of my own turmoil that serves only to deepen the rift between us. And yet, despite the pain of her betrayal, I cannot deny the pull of the past, the memories of a childhood spent together, of laughter and friendship that now seem like distant echoes of a bygone era.

"Isabella," I breathe, my voice barely above a whisper as I take in her familiar face, the years melting away in an instant as I meet her gaze. "It's you."

My parents share a knowing glance, their expressions alight with joy as they turn to face her. "Isabella," my mother says, her voice filled with warmth and affection. "We never thought we'd see you again. We're so happy you're here. I have thought about you so much since your father passed away. I have wondered how you were. I was so upset when your stepmother wouldn't continue to let you come by after your father married her," my mother continues as she holds her arms open to pull Isabella into a hug.

Tears well up in Isabella's eyes as she steps forward, her hands trembling slightly as she reaches out to embrace my mother. "Thank you," she whispers, her voice choked with emotion. "It's been too long."

As we stand together in the warmth of the palace, surrounded by the love and support of my family, I can't help but feel a sense of overwhelming gratitude wash over me. For years, I've longed for a connection and the connection that Isabella and I had as kids is going to be that foundation that we can easily build on.

My father clears his throat, drawing our attention back to him as he smiles warmly at Isabella. "We're thrilled to see you again, Isabella," he says, his voice filled with genuine happiness. "And even more thrilled to see that you and James have found each other after all of these years and for you two not to be the childhood friends that we remember, but we couldn't ask for a better wife for our son."

Isabella's cheeks flush with color as she meets my gaze, a shy smile playing at the corners of her lips. "Thank you, Your Majesty," she replies, her voice soft but filled with sincerity.

In that moment, surrounded by the love and support of my family, I have a rush of emotion that this is meant to be. It will be the childhood friendship and the fact that we were meant to find each other that will make things easier for her to step into my world, both of my worlds, the royal and the BDSM worlds.

Later that night, as I lie alone in my room thinking about Isabella being down the hall in her room, which she insisted on having so that we could date even though my parents are ready to walk us down the aisle, the weight of my emotions pressing down upon me like a suffocating blanket. I cannot help but remember the days we spent together as children. The hours we whiled away exploring the palace grounds, the secrets we shared beneath the canopy of the stars.

But now, as I lie in the darkness, alone with my thoughts, I am angry that Isabella didn't reveal her true identity before my parents saw her. But despite the pain of her deception, I cannot help but wonder what her real reason was and know that if it was fate for us to be together then it doesn't matter that she held it from me.

CHAPTER ELEVEN

Isabella

I WAKE UP THE next morning with so much on my mind. I need to ask Prince James for a favor. I got ready and went to the dining room for breakfast. After we finished eating, Prince James and I headed out to the gardens where we used to play.

I stand before Prince James, my heart racing with anticipation and uncertainty; I steel myself for the conversation that lies ahead. His gaze is steady, unwavering, as he waits for me to speak, and I know that the time has come to lay bare my deepest fears and desires.

"Prince James," I begin, my voice trembling slightly with nervousness, "I have something to ask of you."

He inclines his head in silent encouragement, his eyes urging me to continue.

"I would like to invite my sisters to the palace to stay with me for a few days," I say, my words tumbling out in a rush of emotion. "I need their support, their guidance, as I navigate the complexities of our...situation."

To my relief, the prince nods in understanding, his expression one of genuine concern. "Of course, Isabella," he replies, his voice soft and reassuring. "Anything you need, I will provide."

With a sense of gratitude flooding through me, I follow him as he leads the way to my room, the weight of my decision heavy upon my shoulders. As I step into the luxurious surroundings of the palace, I cannot help but marvel at the opulence that surrounds me—the sumptuous furnishings, the elegant decor, a stark contrast to the modest surroundings of my childhood home.

But even as I marvel at the splendor before me, my thoughts are consumed by the daunting task that lies ahead. Lady Helena's reaction to my new-found status as the prince's chosen bride weighs heavily upon my mind, filling me with a sense of dread and foreboding. I can only hope that my sisters will be able to offer me the support and guidance I so desperately need as I navigate the treacherous waters of courtship and marriage.

Later that day, as Anna and Dressie arrive at the palace, I cannot help but feel a surge of relief at the sight of their familiar faces. We embrace tightly, our tears mingling as we share the weight of our shared burden, and I know that I am not alone. That no matter what lies ahead, I will always have my sisters by my side.

Over the course of the next few days, we talk late into the night, sharing our hopes and fears, our dreams and desires. We speak of the challenges that lie ahead, of the uncertainties that cloud our future, and yet through it all, I feel a sense of strength and determination growing within me, a resolve to face whatever may come with courage and grace.

After they leave and head home, I make my way into the palace and head upstairs to his room. I knock on the door, but he doesn't answer so I let myself in. I didn't see him anywhere, so I head into his closet and open the secret door.

I walk into his playroom and walk up to the bed. I run my hand across the satin sheets. I walk over to the whipping horse and stare at it for a minute before heading over to the ropes hanging from the ceiling. That's when I hear the door to the room close. I turn around, and he is standing there drying his hair with a towel, buck as naked. *Damn, the body on this man.* My eyes stroll down his hard abs to his dick, and my pussy got immediately wet. I raise my eyes to see him grinning at me.

"Like what you see, Izzy?" he asks.

I can't speak; I just stood there. Finally, I clear my throat, "I have made my decision. I will become your wife, and I will trust you to guide me as I explore this new world of yours, the world of BDSM."

He doesn't say anything. Just walks up to me.

"Trust me," he says.

I shake my head yes as he walks over to me, grabs my hand, and takes me out to the bedroom.

"Sit right here. I will come get you when I am ready," he says.

Prince James

I take her hand, and as I lead her into the dimly lit room, the scent of leather and candle wax hanging heavy in the air, I know that this moment will shape the course of our relationship forever.

"Welcome to the dungeon, Isabella," I say, my voice low and steady as I gesture toward the array of equipment that lines the walls. "We are going to start exploring the depths of your desires, where you will learn to trust me completely."

Her eyes dart around the room, taking in the sight of the various implements once again: the St. Andrew's crosses, the padded benches, the racks of floggers and paddles. And though I can see the uncertainty flicker in her gaze, I also see a spark of curiosity. It is the same spark that drew me to her in the first place.

"Tonight, I going to test your levels a little," I continue, my voice soft yet commanding. "I am going to give you a taste of the pleasures that await you in this lifestyle. But remember, Isabella, you are always in control. You have the power to stop at any time, to say no if something doesn't feel right."

"Take off your clothes," I say.

I see the look of hesitancy and nervousness. That's when I realized that not only is BDSM new to her, but being with a man is, too. *Damn, I am about to really push her limits.*

As she removes her clothes, I think about how beautiful and how brave she is. When she is done, my dick stands at attention. I take her hand and lead her to the center of the room, where a padded bench awaits us. As she hesitates, I squeeze her hand in mine, my touch gentle yet firm as I guide her into position, securing her wrists and ankles with soft leather cuffs.

"Relax, Isabella," I murmur, my voice a soothing balm against her nerves. "Trust me to take care of you, to show you the pleasures that await when you surrender yourself to me."

And then, as I begin, I let go of all pretenses, allowing myself to fully embrace the role of her Dom. With each stroke of the flogger, each caress of the whip, I can feel her body respond, her gasps and moans music to my ears.

But amidst the pleasure, there is also a deeper connection, a bond that transcends the physical, linking us together in a way that defies explanation. And as I look into her eyes, I see a flicker of understanding, a recognition of the trust that exists between us, the trust that will guide us on this journey together.

When I release her from her restraints, my touch is gentle as I help her to her feet. And as she stands before me, her cheeks flushed with arousal, I know that this is only the beginning, that together, we will explore the depths of our desires, forging a connection that will last a lifetime.

I pick her up and tote her to the bed, where I lay her down and make love to her for the first time, making sure to take it easy and care for her every need.

Epilogue

Isabella

As I stand before the mirror in the grand chamber of the palace, the excitement and anticipation of the day ahead wash over me in a wave of emotions. Today is my wedding day, a day I never imagined would come, yet one that fills me with a sense of overwhelming joy and gratitude.

Six months have passed since that fateful night at the Royal Play Party, where I met Prince James as an adult, and I embarked down this path that would forever change the course of my life. In that time, I have come to know him as a grown man in ways I never thought possible, to love him with a depth and intensity that surpasses anything I could have imagined.

As I gaze at my reflection in the mirror, I can't help but feel a sense of disbelief at how far I've come. Growing up in the palace where there are so many memories of James and me playing in the garden and getting in trouble for stealing cookies from the kitchen. Even then, I never dreamed that one day I would be standing here, preparing to marry James and become a part of the royal family.

But here I am, surrounded by the opulence and grandeur of the palace, preparing to embark on a new chapter of my life with the man I love by my side. And as I take in the sight of Elizabeth, Anna, and Dressie bustling around me, helping me prepare for the day ahead, I can't help but feel a sense of gratitude for my family.

"Are you ready, Isabella?" Elizabeth asks, her voice filled with warmth and affection as she adjusts the veil in my hair.

I nod, a smile playing at the corners of my lips as I meet her gaze in the mirror. "More than ready," I reply, my voice filled with excitement and anticipation.

As the final touches are made to my hair and makeup, I can't help but feel a sense of nostalgia wash over me as memories of my childhood here at the castle flood back. It feels surreal to be back in these familiar surroundings, surrounded by the people who have become like family to me.

And as I make my way towards the grand hall, where James awaits me at the altar, I am filled with a sense of peace and contentment unlike anything I have ever known. For in this moment, surrounded by love and surrounded by family, I know that I am exactly where I am meant to be.

As I walk down the aisle, my heart pounding with excitement, I can feel the eyes of everyone in the room upon me. But it's the sight of James waiting for me at the end of the aisle, his eyes filled with love and adoration, that fills me with a sense of overwhelming joy.

And as the King himself takes my arm and leads me toward my prince, I know that this is the beginning of a new life filled with love, laughter, endless possibilities, and a lot of kinky sex and parties! As we exchange vows and pledge our love to each other in front of our family and friends, I know that this is where I am meant to be.

About the Author

Ireland Lorelei

She is from a small coastaltown in North Carolina and currently resides in Florida. She started reading romance novels, watching soap operas and romance/drama movies with her motheras a teenager. She then started enjoying horror, mystery, and thrillers. Herimagination and creativity started her to write her own romance novels. Ireland started writingcontemporary romance and contemporary with a little erotica and spread her wings into dark romance, reverse harem and paranormal romance.

https://linktr.ee/irelandlorelei

MASQUERADE PARTY

Ireland Lorelei

Brody Carter is Jason's little brother. He followed his bigbrother's footsteps and joined The Powerful & Kinky Society as soon as heturned eighteen. While in college him and his frat brothers Chaz and Jaxson createdFetish Freaks, a social media platform to bring those with like kinks andfetishes together.

Chaz Rogers knew nothing about the lifestyle until he metBrody. Jaxon Santos had dabbled a little bit in the lifestyle but got heavyinto it when he and Brody became best friends. When the three of them createdFetish Freaks, Chaz and Jaxon joined Brody in The Powerful & Kinky Society.

Three years after starting Fetish Freaks, the guys start anew venture that allows for the local members of the social media platform tomeet and explore their kinks in a safe environment. They built The Fourth BaseDungeon. It was an open floor plan with three bars, ten beds and all the BDSM-toys anyone could ask for.

On opening night of The Fourth Base Dungeon in walks actressMelody Remington. All three men are infatuated with her and decide to all tryto make her their sub. They had always said that no woman would come betweentheir friendship so sharing women was nothing new to them. The task here iswill she want them all, or just one of them, or neither of them.

THE SPICE CLUB

Ireland Lorelei

Allison Cramer has been in the BDSM lifestyle for almost a year. Lucas, a Billionaire and member of ThePowerful & Kinky Society, is her first Dom. Eight months into the contract,Lucas starts to shows his true colors and Allison is not having fun anymore. Onenight he takes it too far and now she isn't sure she can continue to live thelifestyle anymore.

Jason Carter, a Billionaire,owner of The Spice Club and board member of The Powerful & Kinky Society meetsAllison through their mutual best friends, Mike and Abby. He wants her to behis new Sub. He asked Mike if she was contracted to anyone and Mike told herthat she was. But when he finds out that it was her that The Society isprotecting from Lucas and what he did to her, he becomes outraged and wantsnothing more than to show this beautiful woman how a real man/Dom treats awoman/Sub.

Can Jason help Allierealize that she can move forward and not all Dom's are like Lucas? In showingher how it is supposed to be, he starts to have feelings for her that he hasnever had before with any woman and definitely not a Sub. How does he handlethese feelings?

www.ingramcontent.com/pod-product-compliance
Lightning Source LLC
Chambersburg PA
CBHW071213130726

47998CB00002B/735